A Visit to
VIETNAM

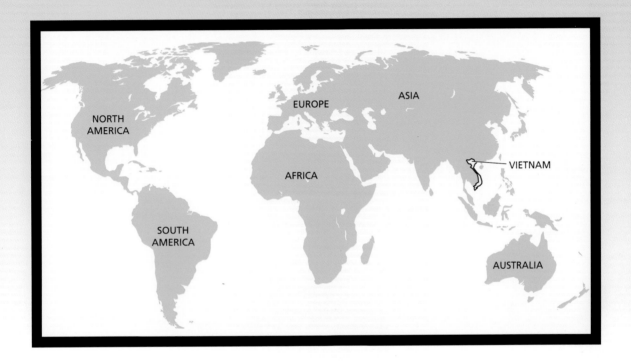

NORTH AMERICA

SOUTH AMERICA

EUROPE

ASIA

AFRICA

VIETNAM

AUSTRALIA

Peter & Connie Roop

Heinemann Library
Chicago, Illinois

© 1998 Reed Educational & Professional Publishing
Published by Heinemann Library,
an imprint of Reed Educational & Professional Publishing,
Chicago, IL

Customer Service 888-454-2279

Visit our website at www.heinemannlibrary.com

Printed in Hong Kong / China
Designed by AMR

02 01
10 9 8 7 6 5 4

Library of Congress Cataloging-in-Publication Data

Roop, Peter.
    Vietnam / by Peter and Connie Roop.
        p.   cm. -- (A visit to)
    Includes index.
    Summary: Describes many aspects of this long, narrrow, southeast
Asian country including its land, landmarks, homes, food, clothes,
schools, sports, celebrations, and arts.
    ISBN 1-57572-120-1 (lib. bdg.)
    1. Vietnam--Juvenile literature. [1. Vietnam.] I. Roop,
Connie.   II. Title.   III. Series: Roop, Peter. Visit to.
DS556.3.R66 1998
959.7--DC21   97-37919
                                                 CIP
                                                  AC

Acknowledgements
The Publishers would like to thank the following for permission to reproduce photographs:
J. Allan Cash: p. 28; Robert Harding Picture Library: p. 9, T. Hall p. 17, T. Waltham p. 11; Hutchison
Library: C. Pemberton p. 8, R. Francis p. 16, S. Murray pp. 21, 23; Link Picture Library: S. Kessler pp. 12,
13, 29, K. Naylor pp. 5, 6, 10, 14, 15, 19, 20, 24, 27; Still Pictures: J. Schytte p. 25; Trip: H. Bower p. 22,
A. Tovy p. 18, Viesti p. 26, B. Vikander p. 7.

Cover photograph reproduced with permission of M. Cuthbert / Spectrum Colour Library.

Our thanks to Rob Alcraft for his comments in the preparation of this book.

Any words appearing in bold, **like this**, are explained in the Glossary.

Contents

Vietnam

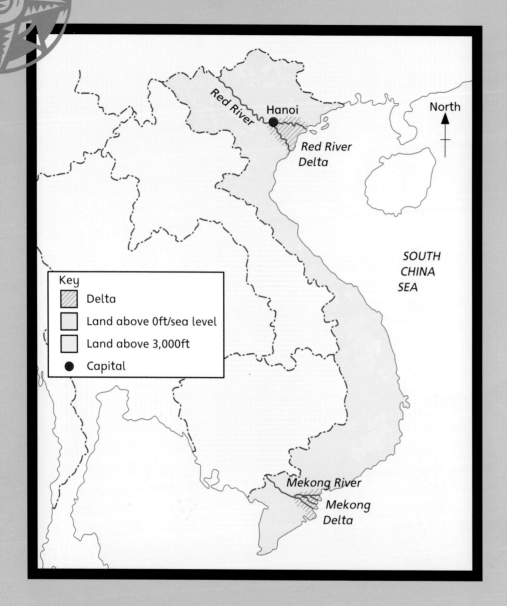

Key
- Delta
- Land above 0ft/sea level
- Land above 3,000ft
- Capital

Red River

Hanoi

Red River Delta

North

SOUTH CHINA SEA

Mekong River

Mekong Delta

Vietnam is in southeast Asia. It is shaped like a giant letter S.

Vietnamese eat, play, and go to school like you. Vietnamese life is also **unique**.

Land

The west of Vietnam has many mountains.
The east of Vietnam is next to the sea.
There are rich, green lowlands in the middle.

In the lowlands, farmers plant rice in wet fields called rice paddies. Heavy rain floods the rice paddies in the **monsoon season**. Farmers need the monsoons for good crops.

Landmarks

Vietnam has two big rivers called the Red River and the Mekong River. These rivers form **deltas,** like this picture, where they run into the sea. Most people live in these deltas.

Hanoi has been the **capital** of Vietnam for almost 1,000 years. Long ago China ruled Vietnam. You can still see Chinese buildings in some places.

Homes

Most Vietnamese people live in small villages. Many homes are made of stone or **bamboo**. Few of these homes have running water or electricity.

City homes are small. People live in small apartments very close together. Grandparents, parents, and children all share the same home.

Food

People in Vietnam often eat food bought from food **stalls**. They eat their meals with **chopsticks** called *duon* (dwan).

Meals are made up of lots of rice. It is put into a bowl with small pieces of vegetables, meat, or fish. *Nuoc cham* (nwahk chom), made from fish, is a tasty sauce.

Clothes

Vietnam has a hot, **humid climate**. Most people wear loose, cool cotton clothes. Straw hats, called *non la* (non lah), are important because of the hot sun.

On special occasions, women wear *ao-dai* (aoh-doy). It is like a long shirt and is worn with pants. Men wear *ao-the* (aoh-theh) which is like *ao-dai* but not as tight.

Work

Most Vietnamese people work in farming or fishing. Rice is the most important **crop**. Fruits and sugarcane also grow well in Vietnam's hot **climate**.

Workers in factories make bicycles, glass, bricks, clothes, and **electronic products**. People also **mine** coal in Vietnam. Coal is used for cooking or it is made into electricity.

Transportation

In the cities, most people travel on bikes, motorbikes, and cyclos. A cyclo is a three-wheeled bicycle. It is the Vietnamese taxi.

Many people travel in boats on the rivers and **canals**. In the country they ride water buffalo. Water buffalo also pull carts and **plows**.

Language

Most people speak Vietnamese. There are also groups of people who speak their own languages and have their own **traditions** and clothes.

The Vietnamese used to write *chu nom* (chew nom) which is similar to Chinese. *Quoc ngu* (kwok-new) is the **modern** way of writing Vietnamese. It uses the English alphabet.

School

In Vietnam, all children go to school from ages six to eleven. They are in school six days a week. They learn to read, write, and do math.

Students have to help their families bring in the **crops**. This is why most schools are closed at harvest time.

Free Time

Most Vietnamese people work all day, for six days a week. When they relax, they play **pool**, soccer, and table tennis. They also like to swim and fish.

Sharing time with family and friends is important to the Vietnamese. They enjoy chess, cards, stories, and music with cups of hot tea or home-made sweets.

Celebrations

New Year, called *Tet*, lasts for a week. Families clean their homes and decorate them with peach blossoms. Food, fireworks, and games make *Tet* an exciting holiday.

People celebrate *Trung Thu*, the Autumn Moon festival, in September. Whole villages spend the day dancing and singing.

The Arts

Vietnamese artists are famous for their jewelry, paintings on silk, and wood-carvings.

Special water-puppet shows can only be seen in Vietnam. The puppets act out well-known stories, on lakes or ponds! People watch from the shore.

Fact File

Name   The full name of Vietnam is the Socialist Republic of Vietnam.

Capital   The **capital** city is Hanoi.

Languages   Most people speak Vietnamese but some can speak French or English, too.

Population There are more than 74 million people living in Vietnam.

Money   Instead of the dollar, the Vietnamese have the dong.

Religions   Most Vietnamese people believe in Buddhism, Taoism, or Catholicism.

Products   Vietnam produces lots of rice, fish, oil, gas, and coal.

Words You Can Learn

chao (chow)	hello
tam beit (tom bet)	goodbye
ban (bahn)	friend
cam on (cam on)	thank you
da (dah)	yes
khong (khum)	no
mot (mote)	one
hai (hi)	two
ba (bah)	three

Glossary

bamboo	a tall plant with a long, strong stem
canal	a river dug by people
capital	the city where the government is based
chopsticks	a pair of sticks held in one hand to lift food to the mouth
climate	the normal type of weather for the area
crop	plants that farmers grow
delta	Sometimes a river slows down and drops lots of mud where it meets the sea. This mud builds up and makes land called a delta.
electronic	using electricity, like computers and televisions
humid	when the air feels damp or wet
mine	dig out of the earth
modern	new and up to date
monsoon season	a time of very rainy weather
plow	tool that farmers use to dig and turn over the soil before planting
pool	a game played on a special table where each player has to hit the right balls into the side pockets
products	things which are grown, taken from the earth, made by hand, or made in a factory
stalls	tables and shelves laid out with things for sale
traditions	ways of doing things that have been done for a long time
unique	different in a special way

Index

More Books To Read

Jacobsen, Karen. *Vietnam*. Danbury, CT: Children's Press. 1992.

Kalman, Bobbie. *Vietnam, the Culture*. New York: Crabtree Publishing. 1996.

Kalman, Bobbie. *Vietnam, the People*. New York: Crabtree Publishing. 1996.